■ Little Learner Bible Story Books ■

Bold Believers in Jesus

From the Book of Acts
for children
by Deborah Henry

Illustrated by
Chris Wold Dyrud

Dedicated to Heather,
John, Andrew,
Nathan, Emily...
my dear nieces and nephews

Copyright © 2005 Concordia Publishing House
3558 S. Jefferson Avenue, St. Louis, MO 63118-3968
1-800-325-3040 • www.cph.org

Scripture quotations are from The Holy Bible, English Standard Version, copyright © 2001 by Crossway Bibles, a division of Good News Publishers. Used by permission. All rights reserved.

This publication may be available in braille, in large print, or on cassette tape for the visually impaired. Please allow 8 to 12 weeks for delivery. Write to the Library for the Blind, 7550 Watson Rd., St. Louis, MO 63119-4409; call 1-888-215-2455; or visit the Web site www.blindmission.org

Manufactured in Colombia

1 2 3 4 5 6 7 8 9 10   14 13 12 11 10 09 08 07 06 05

Jesus told His apostles that He was going back to heaven to be with His Father. He promised that they would not be left alone.

Very soon, He sent them the Holy Spirit. People heard a sound like a mighty rushing wind. They saw tongues of fire resting on the apostles.

God

Life

The Holy Spirit gave the apostles the words to say about Jesus, so that when they preached, the people were filled with the Holy Spirit. Three thousand people were baptized.

The people were filled with the Holy Spirit.
The Lord added more believers to His Church.

Forgiven

Faith

Christian

Peter, John, Philip, and the other apostles healed people in the name of Jesus.

The believers, called Christians, sold land and houses. They brought the money to give to the people who needed help. They fed the hungry.

Christians worshiped together, ate together, and prayed together. They asked God to help them speak boldly about Jesus and heal people in Jesus' name.

One time when they prayed, the whole place shook. God answered their prayer. They were all filled with the Holy Spirit. They kept speaking God's Word boldly.

The people were filled with the Holy Spirit.
The Lord added more believers to His Church.

God   Christian

Sometimes the Christians were afraid they would be thrown into jail because they believed in Jesus, their Savior. The apostles were put in prison. They said, "We must obey God rather than men." They spoke God's Word boldly.

God

Forgiven

Once an angel of the Lord opened the prison doors and set them free. The apostles went back to the temple to preach and teach Jesus, the Christ.

The people were filled with the Holy Spirit. The Lord added more believers to His Church.

Life

Christian

Faith

Stephen believed in God. The Holy Spirit gave him power to do amazing things among the people. He told people all about Jesus, the Savior. Stephen was filled with the Holy Spirit.

Some church leaders did not want him to preach. They picked up many stones and kept throwing them at Stephen. Before he died, he asked Jesus to forgive their sins. He asked Jesus to take him to heaven.

After this, the Lord added more believers to His Church.

God

Faith

Forgiven

The people were filled with the Holy Spirit. The Lord added more believers to His Church.

Christian

Life

God wants all people near and far, young and old, black and white to know about Jesus, the Savior. The Holy Spirit sent Peter to visit Cornelius, who was different from Peter.

Peter told Cornelius and his family that Jesus died on the cross to forgive their sins too. Peter baptized them.

God

Faith

The people were filled with the Holy Spirit. The Lord added more believers to His Church.

Forgiven

Life

Christian

God

Forgiven

Faith

God chose Barnabas and Paul, who once was called Saul, to boldly speak God's Word. They were filled with the Holy Spirit. They traveled near and far to tell people about Jesus' love and forgiveness. They preached that Jesus is the Way to heaven. Paul wrote letters to the Christians he had visited, telling them more about Jesus, their Savior.

The people were filled with the Holy Spirit. The Lord added more believers to His Church.

Life

Christian

The Lord adds more believers to
His Church today when faithful pastors
baptize and preach God's Word to the
people. In His Word and in Baptism,
God gives us His Holy Spirit.

God

Faith

He gives us faith to believe in Jesus, our Savior.
The Bible tells us that Jesus was born to save us.
He died on the cross to take away our sins. Because
Jesus rose from the dead, we will live with Him forever.
Because the Holy Spirit fills us, we can tell others about
our Savior, Jesus.

**The people were filled with the Holy Spirit.
The Lord added more believers to His Church.**

Forgiven

Christian

Life

Growing Faith

Find the pictures or words that help our faith grow.

HOLY SPIRIT

GARDENER

PASTOR

LORD'S SUPPER

GRACE

"They were all filled with the Holy Spirit and continued to speak the word of God with boldness." Acts 4:31b

Baptism

Cross

Holy Spirit

Holy Communion

Bible